Chocolate, Tea and Coffee

Does chocolate grow on trees?

THE WORLD OF FOOD

You can eat it, drink it, put it in cakes, mix it in milk, make ice-creams with it... But just what is chocolate?

You can't have chocolate without cocoa!

Chocolate comes from the cocoa tree, a plant which flowers all year round. The flowers grow straight out of the trunk and the main branches, and ripen into large fruits: the cocoa pods. One cocoa tree may have seventy pods or more a year. Each pod contains about thirty or forty seeds wrapped in a white pulp: these are the beans. They taste very bitter.

Inside a cocoa pod

The cocoa beans, removed from the pulp

The earliest recipe for cocoa: "xocoatl".

A long time ago, in Mexico, "xocoatl" was the favourite drink of the Aztec Indians. Cocoa beans were grilled, then crushed and mixed with maize flour, pepper, vanilla and water. When Cortez arrived in Mexico with his Spanish soldiers, he tasted this nourishing but rather bitter drink. He liked it so much that he sent a boat back to Spain entirely packed with cocoa beans.

The Aztecs used the dried beans as money. Ten beans bought you a rabbit.

In 1519, the Aztec Emperor Montezuma welcomed Cortez by offering him cocoa pods.

A fashionable drink

Cooks at the Spanish Court thought the drink needed to be less bitter, and added sugar instead of pepper. It was an instant success! But they couldn't keep the recipe secret for long. All over Europe drinking chocolate became the new fashion among the rich and elegant. People would meet to drink chocolate and talk with their friends. Doctors even recommended it to their patients, saying it would make them stronger.

The first chocolate manufacturers

Menier, Lindt, Fry, Cadbury... founded the first chocolate factories. It is only in the last hundred years or so that chocolate has become cheap and easy to buy.

For a long time chocolate was sold as a medicine by apothecaries.

Cocoa trees grow in hot, damp climates and
live for 30 to 40 years.

How are cocoa trees grown today?

Cocoa trees are very tender: they enjoy
warmth and dampness, but they don't
like to be under the burning sun, or to
be in the wind. They have to be
protected all the time, and particularly
when the plants are young. That is why
the young plants are grown in seedbeds
in the shade. From four to eight months
later, the saplings are replanted out of
doors, under an 'umbrella' of tall trees
such as banana trees.

At four to five years old the cocoa trees
have grown fairly strong and need less
shade. When they grow wild in the
forest they can be 10 to 15 metres high,
but in plantations they are trained to be
only 4 or 5 metres high, to make it
easier to harvest the pods.

Kinkajous and monkeys living in the forest adore eating cocoa.

Cocoa pods are also the favourite food of rats and parrots, but in the big plantations the cocoa trees are guarded so that the crop is not eaten.

Cocoa pods are harvested by hand.

When they are ripe they are a beautiful red or orange colour. Once picked, they are sliced in half with a special knife: a machete. The beans are picked out of the white pulp by hand.

The plants are treated with insecticides to stop ants and caterpillars eating the leaves.

How do cocoa beans come to taste of chocolate?

The beans ferment: they are left for a week in large chests, covered with damp banana leaves, and shaken every day.

It is then that they turn brown and take on their special taste.

After they have fermented, the beans are spread out to dry in the sun on large trays for a week or two. The workers turn them over regularly to make sure that they all dry out properly. If it rains the trays can be slid back on the runners and put under cover. Once dry, the beans keep well and don't go mouldy.

It takes almost all the harvest from one cocoa tree to make 20 bars of chocolate.

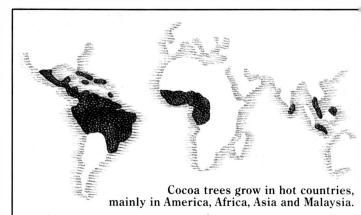

Cocoa trees grow in hot countries, mainly in America, Africa, Asia and Malaysia.

The travels of a cocoa bean

You can tell when a cocoa bean is properly dried: it cracks when you squeeze it in your hand. When the beans are thoroughly dry, they are packed into sacks and put on board ship. The ships leave from ports on the coasts of countries in Africa and South America. The beans go from the lands where they have been grown to the lands where they will be made into chocolate and eaten. They travel to Europe and North

America, to the big chocolate factories.

Machines fill the moulds with chocolate. The moulds
are chilled and the bars turned out.

In the chocolate factory

The beans are cleaned. Then they are
grilled to crack their shells and to bring
out their full flavour. Machines crunch
them until they have turned into a bitter
paste. Then the paste is pressed to
squeeze out all the fat: this is called
cocoa butter. To make chocolate, cocoa
paste, cocoa butter and sugar are mixed
together and stirred all the time for two
or three days. White chocolate is made
by not putting in the cocoa paste.

You may like drinking chocolate best, but grown-ups often prefer drinking tea or coffee. All three drinks contain a chemical called caffeine which helps to stop you feeling tired. They all come from plants which grow in hot climates.

Tea flower

The Chinese were the first tea drinkers.

There is a story that, 4,000 years ago, there was an Emperor of China who sat down under a tree to boil a pot of water. A few leaves drifted down and fell into the pot. They made the water taste delicious. They were tea leaves. Bit by bit, tea became a drink that was enjoyed all over China. About 2,000 years later, the Japanese also discovered tea. Since then, the Chinese and Japanese have drunk tea every day.

In Japan, tea drinking can sometimes be made into a ceremony.

Pekoe, a kind of tea leaf, means in Chinese down or hair.

Tea leaves are picked by hand one by one.

They have to be selected one at a time. The ones which make the nicest tea are called pekoe: they are the young leaves, fresh and juicy, covered in fine down, right at the end of the stalk. The next four or five leaves along the stalk are worth picking, too, but none of the others, which are too tough. Harvesting is done all year long. After they've been picked, the leaves are spread out, dried, turned and heated. Gradually they go brown. Sometimes they are flavoured with flowers: jasmine, orange-blossom, roses...

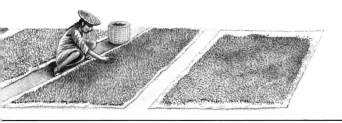

The travels of a tea leaf

How did tea get to Europe? In the sixteenth century, by boat: Dutchmen, travelling to Japan, brought back the first chests of tea. All Europe liked tea, but it was especially popular in England.

It was the English who planted the huge tea plantations in India and Sri Lanka. Since that time, India has become the largest tea producer in the world.

Here is the sort of sailing-ship which was used by the East India Company. It was called a tea clipper, and sailed very fast.

When they are ripe, coffee berries look like little red cherries. They contain two green coffee beans.

The story of coffee

It is said that coffee was discovered hundreds of years ago by shepherds in the Yemen. They noted that their goats became very lively after eating a particular plant which the shepherds did not recognise. The shepherds were puzzled and told their priest.

All together, the shepherds and priest followed the goats, and picked some berries from the unknown plant. They dried the berries and made a drink from them, and then they too found that they became very lively, and couldn't sleep a wink all night. Later on, travellers and pilgrims tasted this desert drink, and introduced it into other countries.

The Yemen is an Arab country.

The habit of drinking coffee spread the world over. In Europe in the seventeenth century it became very fashionable, and people would meet in 'coffee houses' to drink coffee and to talk with their friends. Even today, you may go to a 'café' – the French word for coffee.

The big coffee plantations

Coffee is grown in Africa and in India. The biggest crops of all, though, come from Brazil, a huge country in South America.

Right up until the nineteenth century, the plantations were worked by slaves brought over from Africa to look after the coffee plants, water the bushes and pick the berries...

Coffee is a sensitive plant: cold, too much rain, or too little, can destroy a whole crop.

Coffee beans before and after roasting.

Beans inside a berry.

Harvesting coffee

When the coffee berries are ripe, they are picked by hand, one by one, or pulled off the bushes using special combs. Once gathered into large baskets, the berries are dried and boiled to release the coffee beans.

The green bean does not smell of anything. It only goes brown and begins to have that special coffee smell after it has been roasted. So that the beans do not lose their flavour, it is best not to grind them until just before making a drink of coffee.

Each kind of coffee has a different flavour: Arabica from Brazil and Colombia is the most popular. African Robusta has a more bitter taste.

A cake you don't need to cook

For this recipe you will need:

200 grammes of plain biscuits, 6 teaspoonsful of
sugar, 150 grammes of chocolate,
125 grammes of butter, 2 egg yolks,
2 soupspoonsful of water.

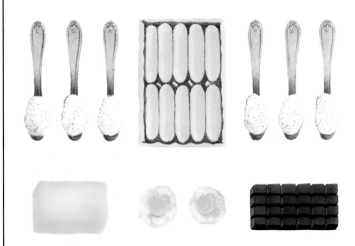

Break up the biscuits and mix with the
egg yolks. Melt the butter and chocolate
together with the water in a saucepan
over a low heat, and then mix them up
with the biscuit mixture. Turn into the
buttered dish.

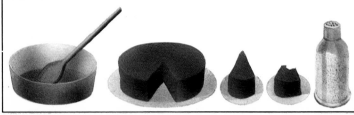

Written by Catherine de Sairigné
Illustrated by Alan Cracknell

Specialist adviser: Robert Press,
Botanical Consultant

ISBN 1 85103 002 6
First published 1986 in the United Kingdom by
Moonlight Publishing Ltd,
131 Kensington Church Street, London W8